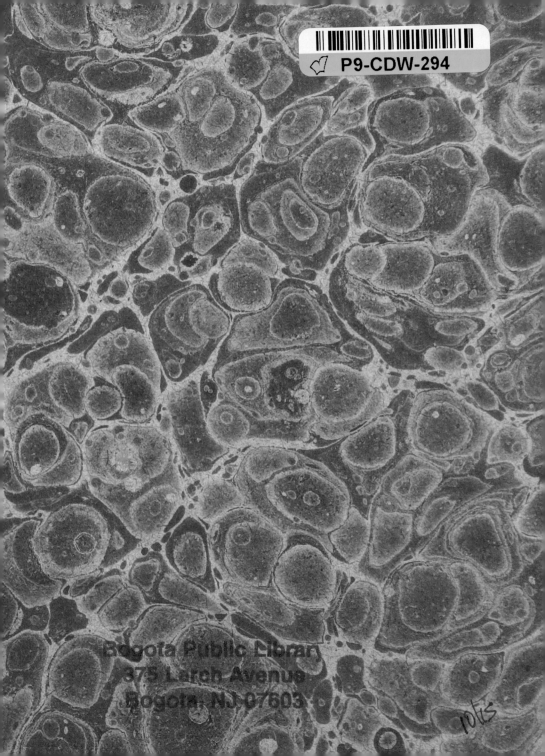

Vimes looked at the cover. The title was
The World of Poo. When his wife was out of eyeshot he
carefully leafed through it. Well, okay, you had to accept
that the world had moved on and these days fairy stories
were probably not going to be about twinkly little things
with wings. As he turned page after page, it dawned on him
that whoever had written this book, they certainly knew
what would make kids like Young Sam laugh until they were
nearly sick. The bit about sailing down the river almost
made *him* smile. But interspersed with the scatology was
actually quite interesting stuff about septic tanks and
dunnakin divers and gongfermors and how dog muck
helped make the very best leather, and other things that
you never thought you would need to know, but once
heard somehow lodged in your mind.
Apparently it was by the author of *Wee* and if Young Sam
had one vote for the best book ever written, then it would go
to *Wee*. His enthusiasm was perhaps fanned all the
more because a rare imp of mischief in Vimes led him
to do all the necessary straining noises.

From *Snuff*

TERRY PRATCHETT

PRESENTS

Miss Felicity Beedle's

The World of Poo

Assisted by Bernard and Isobel Pearson

Doubleday

NEW YORK · LONDON · TORONTO · SYDNEY · AUCKLAND

Copyright © 2012 by the Estate of Terry Pratchett, Lyn Pratchett, and the Discworld Emporium

All rights reserved. Published in the United States by Doubleday, a division of Penguin Random House LLC, New York. Originally published in Great Britain by Doubleday, an imprint of Transworld Publishers, a division of Penguin Random House Ltd., London, in 2012.

www.doubleday.com

DOUBLEDAY and the portrayal of an anchor with a dolphin are registered trademarks of Penguin Random House LLC.

Terry Pratchett® and Discworld® are registered trademarks.

Library of Congress Cataloging-in-Publication Data
Pratchett, Terry.
Miss Felicity Beedle's The world of poo / by Terry Pratchett ; assisted by Bernard and Isobel Pearson.
pages cm
"Originally published in the UK by Doubleday, an imprint of Transworld Publishers, a division of the Random House Group Limited, London, in 2012"— Copyright page.
ISBN 978-0-385-53824-4 (hardcover) — ISBN 978-0-385-53825-1 (eBook)
[1. Feces—Fiction. 2. Collectors and collecting—Fiction. 3. Grandmothers— Fiction.] I. Pearson, Bernard, 1946– II. Pearson, Isobel. III. Title. IV. Title: World of poo.
PZ7.P8865Mi 2015
[Fic]—dc23
2014047797

Cover artwork and interior illustrations by Peter Dennis

MANUFACTURED IN THE UNITED STATES OF AMERICA

1 3 5 7 9 10 8 6 4 2

First United States Edition

To young Sam
from

Felicity Beedle

FOREWORD AND
HOPEFUL NOTE TO PARENTS
BY MISS FELICITY BEEDLE,
AUTHOR

What to tell children about the reality of the human world is always a subject very close to the thoughts of all parents; traditionally, requests from young ones for enlightenment as to where babies come from can be steered in the direction of the stork and the gooseberry bush with no great harm done. Although, of course, when the child is, shall we say, of the age to understand, the parent should make haste to see that they are fully informed. In a well-run household this ought to be achievable without too much blushing, if the parents are sensible.

However, I fervently believe that not to talk to

children about what goes into and out of their bodies is to let the subject become furtive with a tendency to cause sniggering. What we eat and subsequently excrete plays a major role in human society and especially in what we are pleased to call civilized society. In my experience the thinking of intelligent parents, faced with the subject, tends to fall between two stools, as it were. Surely we can do better than saying it's nasty?

Our touchstone here is the commonality of mankind: kings and queens and even the likes of our own Lord Vetinari have to eat and excrete. Why should this be a subject of comment or mirth to anyone? Therefore, I decided that young Geoffrey might have a little stroll through what we may call the underside of our world, facing it with interest, curiosity, and common sense; after all, one man's waste is another man's compost. On this particular point, I must say that I was brought up in the countryside where, on a weekly basis, the night soil was buried in the garden, in an area set aside to be the recipient. I can recall, along with many of my countryfolk, that tomatoes would grow on that site the following year without anyone having to make shift to plant them. And what marvellous tomatoes they were!

As they say, what goes around comes around, although you don't have to look at it as it floats past. But acting like a cat and believing that if you can't see it, then it's not there is no way for polite society to behave. Without muck, without dung, there would be no agriculture and without agriculture there would be no people worth talking about.

And so I dedicate this book to my old friend Sir Harry King, a man who can turn dung into gold!

ARRIVING FOR THE
FIRST TIME IN ANKH-MORPORK

It was a long journey for young Geoffrey from his home in the Shires to his grandmama's house in the big city of Ankh-Morpork. For the first time in his life he was travelling alone in the coach and he sat, looking out of the window, feeling a bit scared but also a bit excited. There had been so much going on at home; Cook had said that Mama was having great expectations. Quite what that meant no one would tell him, but he did know he'd been moved out of his nursery and was promised a whole new room of his own with space to keep his model boats and his collection of interesting sticks and potato-shaped objects, which was some consolation. And Papa was always busy going off to foreign places on 'business,' which meant that he was hardly ever there. The upshot of all this was a suggestion

that Geoffrey visit his grandmama while developments took place.

The landscape gradually changed from hills and forests and farms to acres and acres of cabbages on either side of the road like an endless greeny-yellow sea.

There was no sound apart from the rumbling of the coach wheels and the occasional soft trumpeting of the horses' farting. What with that and the cabbages, Geoffrey's world became quite a smelly place. If greeny-yellow could have a smell, Geoffrey thought, it would smell like this, as if the whole world had farted at once.

He knew he was getting near the city when the smell changed to that of woodsmoke and sooty chimneys and, more than anything else, something a bit like the gardener's outdoor privy at home.* If this smell could

* The simplest form of privy is a hole in the ground. Mankind, being ingenious, especially where it leads to reducing discomfort, soon devised easier ways of aiming over a hole in the ground without coming directly into contact with the cold earth. The idea progressed to building small sheds with a nice comfy seat with a hole in it, or even two or three holes for convivial occasions. And thus the basic domestic privy was invented.

In hot weather it was a rich olfactory experience, which enabled the user to find the place on a dark night and without a candle. In the circumstances, this was probably a good thing if it was a very old and ripe privy, because no one should be standing anywhere near it with a naked flame. In cold weather there was less impact on the nose, but the nether parts could well be exposed to a chilly draught, and proceedings were often hasty and unsatisfactory.

Sooner or later a hole in the ground, even if constructed carefully, would fill up. One solution was to move the privy and leave the hole behind. Eventually, the privy would have moved so far that a trip to the Chapel of Easement might involve a walk of several miles and a packed lunch. The other option was to empty the privy. An intrepid band of craftsmen emerged; their sole job in life was to empty privies and dispose of their contents. These faecal heroes were known as night-soil men or gongfermors, and we shall meet them briefly later. They didn't have many friends, except for those of the same occupation . . . However, they were well respected and as they walked down the street everyone would very quickly step out of their way and let them pass.

have a colour, thought Geoffrey, it would probably be brown.*

The coach rumbled through the Least Gate and Geoffrey saw, for the first time, City Watchmen in uniforms, dray horses pulling massive high-sided carts, and tall buildings looming up and blocking out the sky. He saw the commotion and hustle of a street market where pedlars and greengrocers and butchers were shouting out their wares: more people in one place than he had ever seen in his life. After a while, the streets lined with plane trees grew wider and quieter, and the houses had gardens and looked quite grand. The coach gradually slowed and stopped and Thomas, the groom, came around and opened the door with a flourish.

'Here we are, young sir. Number five Nonesuch Street, your grandmama's house.'

Geoffrey climbed down onto the wide pavement and looked up at the tall house. There were railings and a gate, and a short path leading to steps up to an imposing front door and portico.† Thomas took him by the hand and together

---

* The good citizens of Ankh-Morpork burn coal, wood, dried dung, and, when no other alternative beckons, anything that can be persuaded to go up in flames. There are forges and foundries along with dye works, tanneries, and slaughterhouses. In fact every smelly occupation you could think of, and some that you wouldn't like to think of. In addition, with so many animals passing through and with so many people staying put, the heavy sullen smell of poo, in all its varieties, is the main melody in which the other smells are merely the high notes.
† Actually, at the time young Geoffrey didn't know it was a portico, but it was a portico all right and the fact that he didn't know it was a portico didn't stop it being one.

they climbed the steps. Thomas pulled the bellpull and there came a distant ringing from inside the house. Geoffrey suddenly felt a little bit frightened. He had, of course, met his grandmama a few times, but only when she visited his home. Such occasions were always preceded by his mama being a bit short-tempered, a lecture on remembering to say please and thank you, a scurrying of maids, a smell of polish, and his papa retiring hurriedly to his study.

The door creaked open and a tall thin figure dressed all in black and wearing fearsome spectacles looked down at

him. He recognized his grandmama, who quickly bent down to give him a kiss before he had time to flinch or pull his head between his shoulder blades like a tortoise. She didn't say, 'My how you've grown' or 'How was your journey?' or even 'How are you?' but she took him by the hand, and said, 'I'm so pleased you've come to stay, Geoffrey. I expect you'd like some cake.'

Standing behind his grandmama in the doorway was a sour-faced maid wearing black and white and looking like a penguin that had inexplicably found a lemon to suck on. 'This is Lily,' said Grandmama. 'She will take you to your room and show you where to wash your hands before we have tea.'

Lily looked so disapproving and unfriendly that Geoffrey was very grateful that she was just the maid and not someone who might be inclined to kiss him. He thought he'd be lucky to keep his nose if she did. He wasn't to know, but Lily's life had been somewhat enriched by being the eldest in a family that otherwise consisted of eleven boys. In her experience small boys were nothing but trouble and the main cause of dirt, untidiness, and noise. In her somewhat jaundiced view, the only difference between small boys and small dogs was that small boys couldn't be left chained up outside.

Lily picked up Geoffrey's small trunk and, indicating that he should follow her, started up a series of narrowing staircases to the very top of the house and a door marked Nursery. Lily opened the door and put down the trunk.

'There's water in the basin for you to wash your face and hands,' she said. 'Don't leave the soap in the water, don't leave the towel on the floor, and don't splash about. When you're done, young master, come straight down to the dining room for tea.' With that Lily left, not exactly slamming the door but closing it, he thought, with a half slam—or perhaps it could be called a sl—, because it bounced back afterwards.

Geoffrey could hardly take in all the treasures he could see in the room. There was a stuffed dragon hanging from the ceiling, piles of old books, a skipping rope which he looked at with a sneer, a very worn teddy bear, and, best of all, a large wooden rocking horse which had a real mane and leather bridle. He was, however, feeling quite hungry and a bit scared of Lily, so after a quick look around and a wash he found his way downstairs to his grandmama and cake.

After tea, Grandmama suggested that Geoffrey might like to explore the garden. She showed him the door to the conservatory, and at the far end of this the small glazed door that led down some steps to a gravelled path between tall hedges. Geoffrey wandered along the path, around a corner, and found himself this time at the top of a large area of lawn and flower beds. In the distance he could see an orchard and a vegetable patch and a collection of old sheds.*

* Once you have one old shed somehow you always end up with another one, and after that anything can happen.

Geoffrey made a beeline towards the sheds. In his experience they were often the most interesting thing in a garden. As he walked under the ancient apple trees he felt something fall on his head. It was heavier than a leaf and was wet but not cold. He put his hand up to feel something slimy in his hair. As he looked with some dismay at the greeny-white mess across his fingers he heard a jolly voice behind him boom, 'Do you know what that is, my lad?'

'No,' said Geoffrey, turning round.

'That's bird poo,' said the voice's owner, who was leaning on a fork, smoking a pipe. 'It's very good luck when a bird chooses to poo on your head,* young shaver, and the first bit of good luck coming to you is a Sto Lat pippin, which is the sweetest apple in the world.'

As he spoke, the old man polished a shiny red apple industriously on his waistcoat before handing it to Geoffrey. 'My name, as writ down on my birth certificate, is Humphrey Twaddle, but no one calls me that nowadays on account of when they do I hits them with my fork. You can call me Plain Old Humphrey. Although I owe it to my ancestors to tell you, young man, that far from meaning a load of old rubbish, twaddle is a valuable ingredient in the making of lemonade. Not many people know that, but now there's one more,' he said. 'I'm the gardener here, and if I were you I'd wipe my hand on the grass over there rather than on that smart white shirt of yours.'

Geoffrey did as he was told and then decided that if bird poo was going to bring him good luck he ought to try

---

* The belief that a bird pooing on your head is good luck is common to many cultures. When you ask why, the ribald reply is often, 'Well, it weren't a cow.' In fact, birds were often perceived as messengers of the gods and their movements (both geographical and biological) as part of some divine plan. Needless to say only those endowed with arcane knowledge could understand the particular message in bird poo. However, it is believed that some Ephebian philosophers stood for hours under trees hoping for 'a message' – which they got, but invariably the message was that they should soon clean their jackets.

Bird poo is one of nature's special garnishes. A bird's insides are cunningly designed to preserve fluid, and the slimy green poo is iced with white solid wee, as every schoolboy knows, or did, back in the days when schoolboys knew such things.

to keep what was left of it. He raced back through the conservatory into the house and looked around until he found a large pair of scissors in a sewing basket. He ran all the way up to the nursery and, peering into a mottled old mirror, cut off as much of the clumpy bird-poo-hair as he could and put it on the windowsill to dry out.

It was beginning to get too dark to see much outside and Geoffrey began to feel a bit lonely. He wandered downstairs to find his grandmama.

'It's been a long and busy day,' said Grandmama from her big armchair, 'and I think it's time for bed. You may take a candle to go up and you may leave it alight if you like. Don't forget to say hello to Mister Lavatory on the way and I shall soon be up to tuck you in.'

Holding his candle, Geoffrey started back up the stairs. He wasn't normally afraid of the dark but the flickering candle-light made strange shadows on the faces in the big old portraits hanging on the walls. He

hurried along the passage
to the big mahogany door
Lily had pointed out earlier
as the water closet. He'd
heard the term before, but
nothing had prepared him
for the fantastic sight that
now met his eyes. Shiny
white tiles glistened like
running water and there was a
large china hand basin with painted
flowers and, at the far end of the room, a
great thronelike construction. This had a huge
wooden seat with a large hole in it and underneath
what looked like a small chest of drawers but without
the handles. A gleaming copper pipe joined the chest to a
vast dark-green tank attached to the wall near the ceiling.
Hanging down from the tank was a long chain finishing in
a round knob. On the tank were letters that he had to think
about and spell out in his head.

The
DELUGE SUPREME
CHAS LAVATORY
& SONS*

* Sir Charles Lavatory is the president of the Guild of Plumbers and Dunnakin
Divers in Ankh-Morpork. Geoffrey will make his acquaintance before too long.

Geoffrey knew in theory the function of this marvel but he was mystified and intrigued by its operation. He worked out that the chain was there to be pulled, but it was too high for him to reach. He could only manage to do so by clambering onto the wooden seat and had to be careful not to fall into the hole. Looking down into the still pool beneath him he gave the chain a sharp tug and was astonished at the torrent of water that rushed into the bowl: a deluge indeed. He was even more amazed when, as the water came down, the chain pulled him inexorably up into the air. He held on tightly and, as gently as he had risen, he was deposited back down onto the seat. Even so, Geoffrey wasn't certain whether he wanted to be lifted up in the air twice in one day, especially when there was bubbling water beneath him. He decided that he needed daylight to get the full benefit of the contraption and, taking his candle, made his way up to his room.

He set his candle on the small table beside the bed, then searched in the usual place—which was, of course, under the bed—for the familiar receptacle known in polite circles as the pot, the po, the necessary, or the gazunder.

His business done, Geoffrey jumped up into the small bed, which had a well-used, comfortable feel about it, and suddenly found himself missing his mother and his bedtime story. But before he had too much time to think, the door of the nursery opened gently and something wonderful happened. A small brown-and-white puppy with stubby little legs, floppy ears, and a frantically wagging tail was pushed into the room. Without further ado, it rushed across the floor, jumped on his bed, and started licking his face. Grandmama followed the puppy into the room and pulled up a chair to the bedside. 'I thought you might be a bit lonely, so I brought you a friend.'

'What's his name?' asked Geoffrey with delight.

'Well, from the little puddle he's just left outside your bedroom door while we were waiting to come in, I think I'd call him Widdler if I were you,' said Grandmama. 'Like you, he's very young and misses his mother, so you'll just have to look after each other. Now, would you like me to read you a story?'

'Oh, yes please,' said Geoffrey, as he settled down under the covers. But with Widdler curled up beside him he was happily asleep within minutes. Grandmama blew out the candle and quietly slipped back down the stairs.

A TRIP TO THE PARK
AND A NEW FRIEND

Very early the next morning Geoffrey ventured back into the water closet. He sat on the seat with his legs dangling while Widdler the dog ran round in circles, unravelling a roll of soft paper, clearly in some kind of dog heaven. Geoffrey felt like a king on his grand throne. Indeed, like many a king, he was perched on the edge precariously, quite concerned that if he wasn't careful he might slip off; in his case, into the great bowl and its contents below. Eventually, the business at hand being finished, Geoffrey was pleased to see he wouldn't have to climb up again to reach the chain because someone had very kindly added a length of cord with a cotton reel on the end so it was low enough for him to reach with ease.

Picking up Widdler, Geoffrey wandered down to the kitchen, hoping to find some breakfast. The big kitchen seemed

empty but, as in many kitchens in old houses, there was a lot of life going on out of sight. There were rats romping along the drains, biting through pipes and the backs of cupboards, and popping up in the sink and through the skirting board. There were all manner of beetles and weevils and spiders and, in the damp corner under the sink, a collection of snails stuck to the wall. As Geoffrey opened a cupboard or two, hoping to find something to eat, he heard a scurrying scratchy sound coming from behind the pantry door. Between a pot of raspberry jam and a large jar of pickled eggs sat a small grey mouse. The mouse looked at Geoffrey and Geoffrey looked at the mouse. The mouse looked at Geoffrey again and then, possibly because it wanted to, or perhaps because it was frightened, did a poo, followed by another one and another one before running off.*

* Because mice are small they can squeeze in virtually anywhere and leave their poo around the house. However, they mostly take up residence in the kitchen and larder where food is stored and prepared. Mouse poo is about the same size and shape as a grain of rice but thankfully it's much darker in colour so can be picked out, not just from carelessly stored rice but also from bags of flour and other staples. Beware the shortsighted cook: not all the currants in the roly-poly pudding grew on a vine. And don't ever eat black rice.

19

Mice are like that. And all that Geoffrey was left with was a number of small dark droppings, which he scooped up. I wonder if mouse poo is as lucky as bird poo, he thought. I must ask Mister Twaddle.

'I wouldn't put that in your pocket if I were you, my dear,' said a friendly voice behind him. 'Let me see what I can find for you.'

He turned round to see a jolly plump woman, standing in front of the old range. 'My name is Hartley,' she said, handing him an empty matchbox, 'and I'm the cook. After you've washed your hands really well, I'll cook you some breakfast. How would you like a nice boiled egg and toast soldiers?'

~

After breakfast, Geoffrey helped Plain Old Humphrey feed the chickens and collect the eggs. 'Some of these eggs must be quite lucky,' said Geoffrey. 'They've got chicken poo stuck to them.'*

Plain Old Humphrey scratched his head. 'Well, there's no doubt that when bird poo lands on your head it brings good luck, but the bird's got to choose, see. Poo may not always be lucky but it's certainly useful. I use it in the garden. Look over here. I mix horse apples and straw in with the garden waste and that rots down to the best compost you will find. And the thing is, you'll also find lots of worms there, who burrow away, pooing to their hearts' content, which helps to break it up and make it good and fine.'†

---

*   Hen eggs quite often have poo stuck to them, as chickens are indifferent about where they poo. In the Agatean Empire the poo is carefully scraped off and turned into soup, but by and large it's best to wash the poo off the egg just before you boil it, especially if, like some people, you use the same boiling water to make the tea.
†   The humble earthworm produces its own weight in poo every day. This amounts to about a gram, which might not seem much except that there are about 500 worms per square metre of earth. This means that over the course of a year, in one small flower bed, they would produce over 180 kilos of poo. It is as well that the Howondaland elephant does not daily generate its own weight in poo or the whole world would quite soon be Howondaland. Worm poo is completely inoffensive and much prized by gardeners and you really wouldn't know if you'd got it under your fingernails, as indeed most gardeners have. Some gardeners have it in their boots, too, especially when attempting that very tricky gardening manoeuvre known as the transmigration of soils.

Geoffrey went to put his hand into the smelly compost heap to find some worm poo. 'No, don't do that,' said Plain Old Humphrey. 'I'm sure I can find something that will make it easier for a likely young lad such as you to start his own poo collection.'

He went off to one of his sheds and Geoffrey heard a clattering and rattling and a nasty boingggg from within.* Plain Old Humphrey emerged with a garden hose wrapped around him like a snake, which he finally managed to fight off and sling back into the shed. He disappeared again before returning moments later with a bucket and spade.

* By law a nasty boingggg must always be the last noise you hear when any humorous search is made in piles of junk. It's the law; no one knows whose law it is but, nevertheless, it's the law.

Taking the spade, Geoffrey carefully excavated a small hole at the bottom of the great heap and uncovered a tangled knot of wriggling pink worms. 'What does worm poo look like?' asked Geoffrey, bending down to get closer to the worms.

'Well, it's quite difficult to spot in there,' said Plain Old Humphrey, 'but see the little curly heaps of soil over here on the grass? That's your worm poo, that is; it's called worm casts.' He brought out a cobwebby old jam jar and trowel for this delicate work, and with a bit of help, Geoffrey carefully transferred a sample of worm poo into the jar.

Meanwhile, Widdler was running in circles and barking at nothing in particular or anything in general. In the vegetable patch Geoffrey could see a large black cat digging a hole. 'What's that cat doing?' he asked.

'That dratted cat,' said Plain Old Humphrey through gritted teeth, 'is digging up my champion leeks again! I'll swing for him, I will.'

'Why is he digging?'

'Because he's doing a poo. And because cats is a bit particular. They like to bury it when they're done, and because they're a bit lazy, they like to bury it where I've already been digging.' As the cat finished its business and stalked off, Geoffrey moved purposefully towards the spot, holding the bucket and spade. 'I'd let that cool down a bit before you dig it up,' warned Plain Old

Humphrey. 'Mark the place with a stick and collect it in a day or so. Pretty strong stuff your cat poo.*

'Look, you must excuse me, lad, I need to pay a visit.' Carefully lighting his pipe and picking up an old copy of the *Almanak*, Plain Old Humphrey made his way to his small personal privy between the compost heaps and the hedge. 'Why don't you take that puppy of yours for a walk in the park?' he called over his shoulder.

'Please may I wait until you come out?' asked Geoffrey, holding up his bucket.

'No, you may not,' replied Plain Old Humphrey firmly. 'There are some things a chap needs to do without being under observation, especially by a small boy holding a bucket. Even if you can't see him, it tends to put you off your stride, so off you go.'

Geoffrey stood on a pile of old seed boxes and, holding Widdler in his arms, looked over the hedge and into the park. 'Shall we go and explore, Widdler?' he said. Widdler wagged his tail so hard with excitement that his whole body shook.

They crawled through a hole in the hedge together, ran

---

* Cats are secretive animals and their poo is so offensive that even they don't like the smell of it, and so they bury it. Cats also get terribly embarrassed if they know you are watching and will turn the other way.

Even witches, who can use most things in creating spells, draw the line at cat poo. The Ting-Tang-Bang cats of the Counterweight Continent are revered for the vicious nature of their poo, which is collected, carefully dried, and then used to make fireworks; and with minute attention to the cats' diet the most skilled practitioners can get you displays of vivid blue, which are notoriously hard to achieve in the field of feline pyrotechnics.

25

across the grass, and chased each other round and round in circles until Geoffrey fell over. Out of the corner of his eye and not far away he saw another dog stop, squat down, and produce a small pile of poo before scuttling off. Geoffrey wished he'd brought his bucket, and was standing looking at the small brown heap, wondering how to get it home, when a voice asked, 'Is that yours?'

'No, I went before I came out,' Geoffrey replied to the owner of the voice, a shabbily dressed urchin with a bucket in his hand.

The boy looked satisfied. 'Well, it's mine then.'

'What? Are you a poo collector, too?' asked Geoffrey excitedly.

'I most certainly am! My name is Louis and I collect dog poo for Sir Harry King. He'll pay me a penny a bucketful if it's well stamped down. Extra, too, if it's white dog poo—that's the very best. We in the business call it the "pure."'

'Is Sir Harry a collector?' enquired Geoffrey with some interest.

'No, he sells it to the tanning yards.'

'Does he buy mouse poo?' Geoffrey went on, fingering the matchbox in his pocket.

'Don't know,' said Louis with a shrug of his shoulders, 'but if there's money in it, Sir Harry King will collect it, trust me. He's got a grand house down at the corner of Dimwell and Grunefair, but he doesn't keep the poo there because Lady King won't let him bring his work home. He collects all the poo in Ankh-Morpork and deposits it in big yards outside the City Gates.'

I'd very much like to meet Sir Harry, thought Geoffrey. He sounds like a very sensible person.

'Right, I'm off to deliver this to Sir Harry's yard now,' Louis declared when the bucket was full and well stamped down.

'Can I help you again tomorrow?' asked Geoffrey.

Louis looked at him sideways. 'Can't afford to pay you,' he said quickly, 'but if you like I'm mostly here in the early mornings when people walk their dogs.

'This is my patch!' he added with pride. 'I fought hard for this. You just ask the Mitchell brothers: they won't try to take it over again, oh no, indeed. It's a dog-eat-dog world, my friend, is the world of the pure, and even if I say it myself,

I'm one of the best. Sometimes I'm there with my trowel before little Fido even knows he's going to go.' And with that, spotting a small straining figure across the park, the lad was away as if he had wings on his heels—although what was really on his heels was probably not wings . . .

Geoffrey and Widdler crawled back under the hedge into Grandmama's garden. Plain Old Humphrey didn't seem to be around so they climbed the stairs to the top of the house with a short diversion on the first-floor landing where Geoffrey tried to look round the back of the suit of armour. When he got to the nursery he saw with dismay that his lucky poo was not on the windowsill where he'd left it, and neither were the scissors.

'Oh no! I've been tidied,' he cried. 'Being tidied' was something that occasionally happened at home, but since the time his most precious stick had been tidied away (leading to long and recriminatory searches in the rubbish bins), he was usually given a bit of warning.

He dashed down to the kitchen again, where Lily the maid was mopping the floor. 'Have you seen my lucky poo?' he asked frantically. 'I left it on my windowsill with some scissors.'

'Is that what it was?' shrieked Lily. 'That's disgustin', that is. I threw it out the window and thems was my best scissors, too. Don't you go bringing any more dirt up into your bedroom, young man, or I'll tell your granny. And what's that on your shoe?'

Geoffrey went back outside hurriedly to find Plain Old Humphrey, who was wandering down the path with the look of a man whose world was now a more comfortable place. 'Lily tidied out my lucky poo,' he said. 'I don't suppose I'll ever be lucky enough to be chosen by a bird again.'

'Never mind, my lad. Just you wander across the park to the

pigeon loft in Dimwell Street, and stand around there for a minute or two. But here's a tip: put a bit of cardboard on your head first, then you can bring it back nice and easy. And I've got an old shed I'm not using where you can keep it safe.'

'Can I keep my mouse poo there as well? Could I make a poo museum? I think poo is very interesting and it is *not* nasty,' he said, his face going red. 'After all, without poo everybody would explode.'

'Of course,' said Plain Old Humphrey. 'I shall ask Hartley if she's got any more spare jam jars. I think they could be quite useful.'

At that point Geoffrey heard his grandmama calling from the house.

'I think it's time for your tea,' said Plain Old Humphrey. 'Better run along if I was you.'

Grandmama met Geoffrey at the back door. 'If you'd like to wipe your feet and wash

your hands really well, Geoffrey, I think there might be cake for tea. But first tell me, what have you been doing today?'

'Well, I've started a collection,' he said breathlessly, 'and Plain Old Humphrey said I could use his old shed for a museum, and he gave me a bucket and spade and a trowel for collecting. And I took Widdler to the park, but I forgot my bucket and we met a boy called Louis. He was collecting dog poo in a bucket for Sir Harry King and he said I could help him again tomorrow.'

'He would be one of Sir Harry's pureboys,' interrupted Grandmama. 'It's a very useful job. But what exactly are you collecting, Geoffrey?'

'Oh, any poo at all,' he said. 'In fact I want to collect every sort of poo there is. Plain Old Humphrey says it can be very useful and it's interesting and sometimes it can be lucky.'

'Are you sure that's what you want to do?' asked Grandmama. 'Your cousin Robert collects stamps. I believe *they* are quite interesting and can sometimes be quite valuable.'

'No, I think I'd rather collect poo,' said Geoffrey without hesitation. 'I don't think anyone else in the world has a poo collection, so mine would be the first proper museum and I could charge people to come and see it.'*

---

* Sadly Geoffrey was wrong in assuming that his was the first poo museum on the Disc. In the Unseen University there is a magnificent conundrum known as the Cabinet of Curiosities and no scholar has yet plumbed its limitless depths. It is believed to contain samples of poo from every living animal and insect in the multiverse, including such exotic species as the phoenix, unicorn, and quantum butterfly. However, scholars are confident that it lacks the poo of the rocking horse, which is thought to be rarer than anything known to humankind.

Much to his surprise, his grandmama gave him a big, if rather strange smile. 'You are a very original thinker, Geoffrey.' She touched the pearl necklace strung around her neck. 'Would it surprise you to learn that these very expensive pearls are the poo of oysters? Given your interesting predilection I shall think carefully about where would be the best places for us to visit while you are staying. Come and see me after breakfast tomorrow and I shall have a plan.'

A VISIT TO THE
DRAGON SANCTUARY

Geoffrey woke up excited. Today was the day that Emma, one of Grandmama's goddaughters, was going to take him to the dragon rescue centre and sanctuary. After breakfast, he put on his best jacket and stood in the hallway with Widdler, ready and waiting. Before long, his patience was rewarded when the bell rang. He opened the front door to a friendly and jolly girl who looked as if she ate hay and enjoyed a good run before breakfast.

'Hello, Geoffrey. I'm Emma,' she said in a booming voice. When he shook hands with her as he'd been taught to do, she gave him a grip he just knew would crack a walnut; he liked her immediately.

'Now, Geoffrey,' she continued, 'your grandmama gave me

five dollars so we could take a cab to Morphic Street. But it's not far and if we walked instead we could buy some sweets on the way. What do you think?'

'Oh yes,' said Geoffrey enthusiastically, 'I'd much prefer to walk. You never know what you might see.'

They set off along Nonesuch Street past some very grand houses and as Geoffrey was admiring them he saw what looked like two ugly stone animals perched on the edge of a roof.

'What are those creatures doing up there?' he asked Emma.

'Oh, they're just gargoyles,' she said. 'If you've got a very big house and a grand piano and a butler and a carriage with your name on it, the next thing is to hire a gargoyle to sit on the corner and make your house look even more important.'

'But what do they do?' asked Geoffrey.

'Well, originally they would have lived on the tops of very old buildings like the Unseen University where they sat in the gutters and fed off what came through in the water. Now many of them are purely ornamental and have to have food left out. Some, I'm told, even allow themselves to be painted and made to hold up shields. They're quite harmless unless you're a pigeon; they hate pigeons.'

Geoffrey waved up at the gargoyles as they continued on their way and thought he got a wave back.

It was not long before they came to a bridge. Geoffrey was amazed at the houses and shops that lined both sides of its crowded carriageway. Some had small rooms sticking out over the river and as Geoffrey watched he saw something fall from one into the river with a splat.

He and Emma squeezed between two buildings and looked down on to the sluggish River Ankh as it crawled its way to the sea. 'It's a bit smelly,' said Geoffrey, 'and why are those people in the boats holding up umbrellas? It's not rain— Oh, I see,' he nodded, as another splash and splatter reached their

ears and the river was further enriched in its passage under the busy bridge.*

'Some people are too mean to pay Sir Harry King to collect their privy buckets and it just goes in the river,' explained Emma, 'which makes it very smelly and extremely unpleasant for anyone going under a bridge.' She added, 'I think they're making a law about it.'

'Does Sir Harry collect people poo as well as dog poo?' asked Geoffrey.

'Sir Harry collects everything; they don't call him the King of the Golden River for nothing,' she added. 'Come along. Let's go and buy those sweets.'

They entered a funny little shop with advertisements in the window for Jolly Sailor Tobacco and Gumption's Snuff and a large sign above the door saying SWEETS. Behind the counter was the fattest man Geoffrey had ever seen. He had a stubbly grey moustache, and was wearing a hat with a tassel, and a brightly coloured woollen shawl. What really caught Geoffrey's attention was the magnificent parrot sitting on his shoulder.

---

* By and large all rivers passing through cities and towns emerge a lot muckier than they start out. The River Ankh is notorious for its crusted, evil-smelling waters—mainly the result of the inhabitants using it as a drain, occasional burial ground, and repository for all manner of ordure. The worst offenders are those who live or work along the bridges. Human nature being what it is, if it's a question of paying someone to remove a bucket of poo from your dwelling or simply sitting above a hole where out of sight is out of mind, the latter option will win every time. In addition, if you're having a bad day there's the small consolation that you can give someone beneath an even worse one, if you time it right.

'Hello, Mister Thwaite,' said Emma. 'May I have some Klatchian Delight, please? And what sweets do you like, Geoffrey?'

Geoffrey cast his eye around the shop, which had shelves of sweet jars from floor to ceiling.

'How about some nutty slack or dragon drops or, if you like, chocolate?' said Mister Thwaite. 'I've just had a delivery of pig pellets for Hogswatch.'

'Wonderful!' said Geoffrey. 'And if I don't eat them all I can put some in my poo collection.'

'Your what collection?'

'I have a poo museum,' replied Geoffrey proudly.

'Well, I never did,' said Mister Thwaite. 'You can have this packet of gnoll berries. Goodness knows what's in them but I can't shift them for love nor money.' He turned and reached up to a high shelf. The parrot squawked but continued to watch Geoffrey with a beady eye.

As Mister Thwaite turned, Geoffrey noticed that the back of his shawl was encrusted with bird poo. 'You must be a very lucky man,' said Geoffrey, 'to have all that bird poo on you. Could I have a bit of that parrot poo for my museum, please?'

'Of course. I like to help a young man with his hobby,' said Mister Thwaite.

And, holding an empty tobacco packet, he let Geoffrey scrape the well-dried encrustation from the fringes of the shawl. Geoffrey put the bags of sweets and lucky parrot poo into his pockets and, having thanked Mister Thwaite, turned to leave. As he opened the door the parrot suddenly sprang into life, flew to its perch, and did one of those little dances that parrots are wont to do and then shouted very loudly, 'NOW PISS OFF.'

Mister Thwaite smiled. 'Don't worry. He only says that if he really likes you,' he said.

Geoffrey and Emma continued on their journey and before long they found themselves looking up at the most impressive gates Geoffrey had ever seen. As they stood there a change in the wind brought a smell of burning and fireworks that hit the back of his throat and made his eyes water. A shower of small sooty particles floated down around them.

'That can't be good,' said Emma. She pushed the gate open in the manner of someone who knew she would always be welcomed, and they made their way into a yard surrounded by a collection of sheds and bigger stone buildings with thick, fortress-like walls. The roofs, however, looked very insubstantial and, in some cases, very new.

'Those are the dragon sheds,' explained Emma. 'If one of the little dears explodes, the blast is channelled upwards. If we're lucky we only lose a bit of roof.'

'What happens if we're not so lucky?' asked Geoffrey, looking anxious.

'Oh, you'll be all right,' she assured him. 'We've got good protective clothing. It's only the people who forget to wear it who lose their hair and eyebrows, and sometimes their fingers.'

They went into one of the smaller sheds, where they met a girl who seemed to be wearing armour from the neck down and held a large helmet in her gloved hands. 'This is Emma,' said Emma. 'Emma, meet Geoffrey.'

'Hello, Geoffrey,' said Emma Two. 'Let's get you and your dog kitted up.' He was lifted up and lowered into big stiff leather trousers that didn't bend at all, and was given big boots and gloves and a helmet. They even found a small helmet for Widdler, making him look like a snail peering out of its shell.

'Let's go,' said the Emmas in unison, and ushered him from the shed into one of the big stone buildings. At first there didn't seem much to look at. There was a series of concrete pens with small, grey-green huddled lumps under piles of sticky ash.

'Why are they all covered in ash?' asked Geoffrey.

'Well, we've not cleaned them out yet because Lady Sybil can usually tell what's wrong with them from the colour and smell of their poo. They'll have been eating quite the wrong thing.'

'What should their poo be like?' asked Geoffrey. 'And can I have some for my poo museum?'

'Well, like I said, in a healthy dragon there's hardly any poo at all. Sometimes it's just a fine ash that floats away in the air.'*

'I wish I could get some dragon poo,' Geoffrey said. 'I want to get poo from every animal in the world so that people can come to my museum and see it all and be amazed.'

---

* When in good health, Draco vulgaris (the herbivorous swamp dragon) produces hardly any waste material at all, because combustion is complete. However, swamp dragons are notoriously susceptible to digestive disorders and if their diet is not strictly controlled, they can become very unstable. The resulting symptoms range from violent explosions to the production of large amounts of black or green ash. Like all immature creatures, baby swamp dragons are unable to completely digest their food.

Draco nobilis on the other hand is a carnivore. This species is particularly fond of virgins, but knights in armour are a bonus because they add a certain amount of roughage to the diet. Draco nobilis poo is like that of any carnivore, but if knights in armour have featured on the menu in the recent past, the dragons excrete small tin roundels not unlike corned beef, but still in the tin as it were.

To compensate for the lack of dragon poo thus far Geoffrey was given a baby dragon to hold. It perched on his hand, blowing smoke rings and then suddenly, without any warning, deposited a small glowing ember on his gloved palm. Geoffrey couldn't believe his luck! He closed his fist around it tightly for the rest of the tour in case one of the interchangeable Emmas decided that Lady Sybil needed to inspect it. When they came to leave, it seemed cool enough to surreptitiously transfer to his jacket pocket.

Geoffrey and Emma One set off back home hand in hand, with Widdler following so close to heel that he was often in danger of tripping them up.

Geoffrey kept looking up at the grand houses, hoping to see a gargoyle. They were not far from home when they reached a very grand mansion indeed with huge curly iron gates and tall stone pillars on either side. His eyes lit up in delight when he noticed that on top of each tall pillar was a genuine gargoyle holding a shield. 'You must get very bored just sitting up there all day. Would you like a sweet?' Geoffrey said to one of the gargoyles.

'It's more than my job's worth,' said the gargoyle,* 'and I don't get off duty until the end of the week. But Old Pediment over at number eight,' he croaked, 'is always on the lookout for interesting tidbits. He's got a sweet tooth, too.'

'If I leave some sweets on my window-sill at number five, do you think he'd find them?'

'Doesn't miss a thing. Old Pediment,

* The word 'said' is used rather carefully here. If you want to know what a gargoyle talks like, imagine having a conversation with a reasonably friendly rock, and if you want to know what they look like, think of those lizards that spend an awful lot of time apparently staring at nothing, and then suddenly there is a movement in the air and something has suddenly become lunch at an extremely fast speed.

he clears all the bird tables this side of the road and I don't just mean the birds' food.'

As they walked away, Emma said to Geoffrey, 'You are funny. No one I know talks to gargoyles.'

'I want to know where they poo. Gargoyle poo would be a very interesting find for my museum.'

Lily opened the door to them when they arrived back at Grandmama's house. 'Wipe your feet on the mat,' she said, wrinkling her nose in distaste. 'And who's got a bonfire going?'

Geoffrey and Emma went into the drawing room to see Grandmama, who was having a cup of tea. 'My goodness,' she said, 'what is that smell? It's as if someone's been letting off fireworks.' Her eyes went straight to Geoffrey's jacket. 'Whatever have you got in your pockets, my boy?' Geoffrey reluctantly extracted the bags of sweets from one pocket. 'Now come on, Geoffrey, you know I mean the other pocket.'

'It's baby swamp-dragon poo for my museum,' said Geoffrey defensively as Emma helped him off with his jacket . while Grandmama extracted the charred ember with the sugar tongs and transferred the hot little nodule to an empty snuff tin. 'He just laid it in my hand.'

'Well, let me tell you that you are going to wash those hands before you eat anything, my boy,' said Grandmama. 'I shall also have to buy you a new jacket before we go to the Guild annual luncheon.'

She gave Geoffrey a severe look from top to bottom and continued, 'Your late uncle Cedric was very much the same. If I remember rightly he had a very large collection of things

that looked like other things; one of the largest such collec-
tions in the world, I've been given to understand.' She made a
tut-tutting noise and added, 'There's no doubt about it,
incongruity runs in this family. Now I think you should take
your new acquisitions down to your museum before it gets
too dark.'

Geoffrey made his way down to the end of the garden,
where in the dusk he saw the shape of Plain Old Humphrey
leaning on a shovel.

'Hello, young man, what have you been up to today?'

'I've had a lovely time,' said Geoffrey. 'I've spoken to a gargoyle and I've been to a sweet shop—would you like one?—
and visited the dragon sanctuary and guess what I've got?'
He opened the snuff tin and showed the contents to Plain Old
Humphrey.

'Ah, that smells a bit like dragons to me. When I was a boy
we had a little swamp dragon to light the fires. But one day

my dad had a bit of an accident and my mum wouldn't have them in the house after that.'

'It's my best poo so far,' said Geoffrey. 'I must put it somewhere really safe so I can label it up tomorrow morning.'

Later that evening, before he got into bed, Geoffrey remembered to take a few lumps of toffee from the crumpled paper bag and laid them out on the windowsill just in case Old Pediment the gargoyle were to drop by.

A TRIP TO THE MENAGERIE
AND CONVERSATION WITH
A GARGOYLE

Geoffrey was used to waking up to birdsong at home, and he'd got used to the early morning sounds of Ankh-Morpork, but what woke him this morning was quite different. A grinding of stone on stone and a crunching sound drew him to the window where, to his delight, he saw a very large gargoyle chewing the last of the toffee he'd left out.

'Don't go away,' said Geoffrey. 'I'm just going to get dressed.'

The gargoyle shuffled along to make room as Geoffrey and Widdler climbed out onto the windowsill to join him.

'I saw you put that toffee out from across the road. I've not had a bit of toffee for a long time, very nice, too.'

'What do you normally eat?' asked Geoffrey.

'Pigeons are good,' munched the gargoyle and Geoffrey hardly liked to draw his attention to the pigeon sitting on his head wearing a very smug expression. But the gargoyle saw him looking and said, 'Ah, that's my decoy; it's no good getting old if you don't get artful. The silly buggers fly over thinking it's a safe roost and Bob's your uncle! A clever chap over in the Street of Cunning Artificers made it for me. In return I go down there every week or so and get rid of all of the pigeons on his skylight.'*

'I'd better go down to breakfast; Grandmama is taking me to the menagerie today. But I hope I'll see you again,' said Geoffrey, crawling back through the window. 'If I can get back to the sweet shop, I'll bring you some more toffee.'

'Thank you, but the old grinding teeth are not what they were,' replied the gargoyle. 'Cake is a favourite, though, especially fruit cake, but not with nuts—they give me the tweaks.'

'There's lots of cake here,' said Geoffrey. 'I'll put some out for you tonight if I can.'

---

* It is suspected that gargoyles are, in fact, a type of troll. Over the years of their exposure to the abnormal magical activity that always surrounds Unseen University they have evolved into mobile and sentient beings. Their diet is varied but the emphasis now is on pigeons. Their alimentary tract, which is a complex U-shaped organ, was originally designed for the digestion of a watery mineral diet that entered the body through the ears. The solids were filtered and digested in the usual fashion while the liquid was extracted and expelled through the mouth. The recent change in food source has resulted in their ears becoming vestigial, and a small and isolated loop of intestine between the ears and throat, not unlike the human appendix, is all that remains. Another result of this change in diet is their ability to move their jaws and even close their mouths, making it much easier to have a conversation with them. Saying that, gargoyles seldom talk about anything but pigeons and how much they dislike them.

~

After breakfast, Geoffrey and Grandmama set out for the Palace.

'I think you should find this very interesting,' said Grandmama. 'I'm sorry we can't take Widdler with us, but they don't allow dogs where we're going.'

Geoffrey knew it would be somewhere important because Grandmama was wearing a large hat that looked like the top of a big boat and Lily had pressed his trousers. After much muttering about the state of them, she'd also polished his shoes.

They travelled by coach up Park Lane, across the Isle of Gods, and over the Brass Bridge. Geoffrey saw several gargoyles perched up high on the buildings and he leaned out of the window to wave at them.

'A gargoyle came to visit me this morning, Grandmama,' he said, pulling his head back in the coach. 'He was very friendly and I've promised him some cake.'

'Do be very careful, Geoffrey. No wandering around on the roof looking for gargoyle poo; I know that's what you're really after.'

The coach pulled up and they entered the Palace grounds by a small side gate. There was a pleasant stroll along a narrow path until they came to a small and mysterious studded door. Without any hesitation Grandmama gave the end of the bellpull, which was in the shape of a snake, a tug. Geoffrey moved quickly behind her, just in case. The door

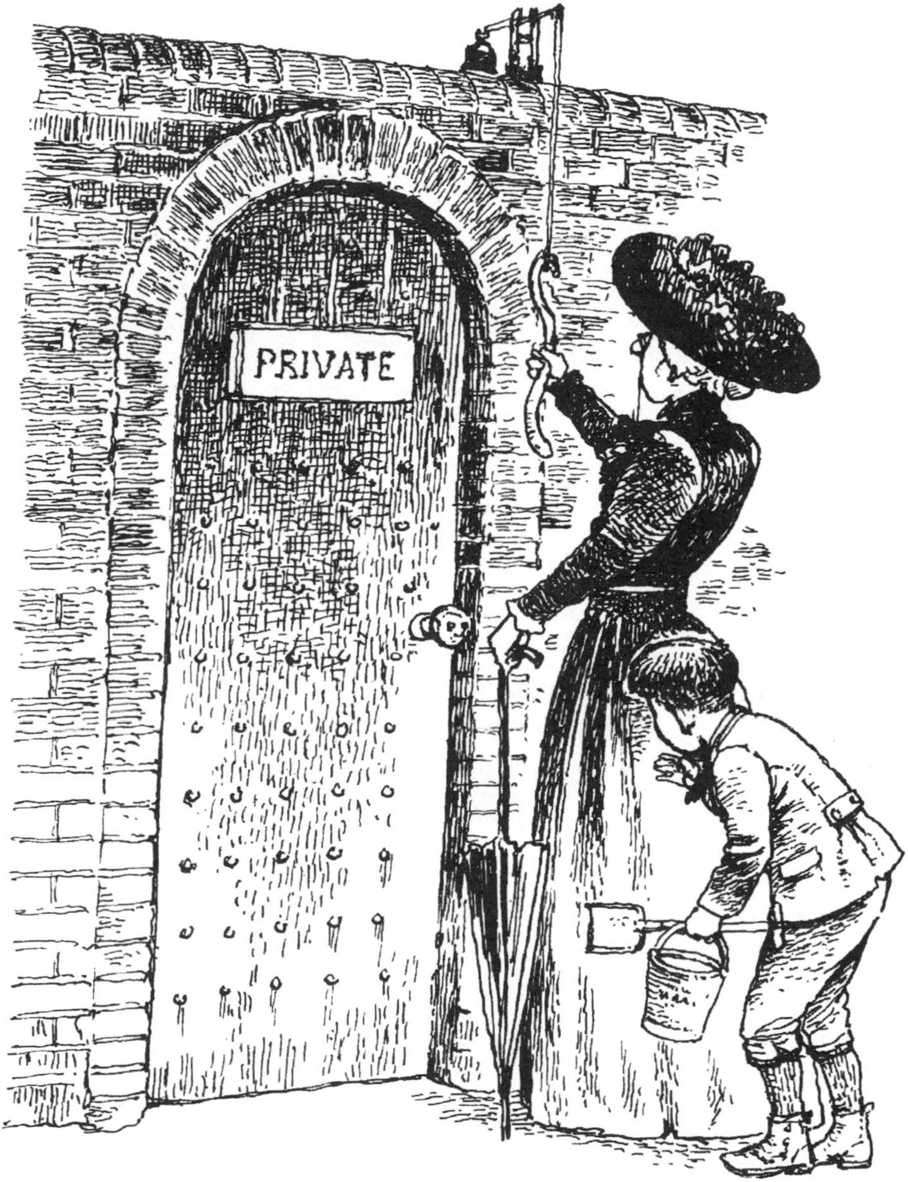
PRIVATE

creaked open to reveal a short man with a very long beard and a flat-peaked cap. He wore tall rubber boots a bit like the ones that Geoffrey had for rainy days, but these were altogether more substantial, the sort of boot that laughed in the face of (or, come to that, the rear of) any animal's nervous activity.

The beard, which seemed to have a life of its own, enquired politely as to who they were and what their business was. Grandmama produced a small card from her pocket. 'We are here at the personal invitation of Lord Vetinari.' The keeper stood to attention, saluted, and a large smile broke the crust between the moustache and beard.

'Good morning, ma'am. My name is Pontoon, with an emphasis on the "oon," and I have the privilege of being his lordship's head keeper. Please do come in, we have been expecting you. What would you like to see first, young man? The largest animal we have here is the Hermit Elephant from Howondaland, and the smallest is the Llamedos Swimming Shrew. We've got Acrobatic Meerkats, Counting Camels, a Ring-maned Lion, a Reciprocating Ocelot—be very careful there—and Dancing Bears, to name but a few.'

'I would very much like to see the elephants first, please,' said Geoffrey.

The old man tapped a finger to his nose and, in the tone of a connoisseur, said, 'Very wise choice, young man, everyone should see the elephants.'

As they walked towards a large enclosure Geoffrey started to explain to the keeper about his poo museum. 'I'd really like to collect some poo from all of your animals. I've even brought my own bucket,' he added.

Mister Pontoon scratched his beard, causing a number of unidentified objects to fall out. 'Well, young man, that is a rare and unusual hobby, but his lordship did say that I was to help you in every way. Your grandmama must be a very influential lady. But it wouldn't be safe for you to go in their cages with your bucket and spade. Besides, all of the poo would get a bit mixed up in just one bucket and you would end up with what we in the industry call miscellaneous poo, and you don't want that.

'I'll ask young Gus—he's the junior assistant keeper—to get the wheelbarrow out. It'll be good experience for him.'

He whistled sharply and a boy of about fourteen, with a shock of straw-coloured hair on which was perched, back to front, an old keeper's hat, emerged from a shed pushing a very official-looking wheelbarrow. He seemed too big for his clothes, with the exception of his boots, which would have fitted a giant.

'We've got some old feed bags,' said Mister Pontoon, 'and there's some waxed-paper bags that my missus puts my sandwiches in. That should do us for now and we can gather your samples as we go, so to speak.'

They followed the boy pushing his barrow to a large enclosure, with a very high fence made of strong iron bars. Inside were a number of tea-cosy-shaped haystacks, some of which seemed to have door openings, showing a dark interior. Quite suddenly one of the haystacks rose up on four stumpy grey legs and began to wander away. When it stopped a huge pile of poo dropped to the ground with a wet splatty sound.

'Gosh,' said Geoffrey, 'I don't think I've ever seen a poo as big as that before. If Plain Old Humphrey were here he'd want that for his compost heap.'*

Geoffrey and his grandmama continued past what they now knew to be elephants to a large cage holding a sulky-looking camel. Unusually, the bars of this cage were horizontal rather than vertical, with large spherical beads threaded at intervals, which the camel listlessly pushed to and fro.

---

* Elephants, including hermit elephants, eat grass, leaves, and sometimes whole tree branches, but absorb only 40 percent of the nutrients. This means that elephant poo not only makes good compost but is also of considerable nutritional value to other animals, especially birds and insects. An elephant can produce about twenty kilograms of poo a day; over a year that would stack up to over seven thousand kilograms. On the basis that an elephant lives for sixty-five years or so, we're looking at a lifetime production of poo not far short of five thousand tonnes, which is, it has been calculated, enough poo to fill the Ankh-Morpork Opera House up to the small trapdoor in the loft.

'That's a Counting Camel from Djelibeybi,' said Mister
Pontoon. 'He gets really bored if we don't keep him occupied.
Careful in there, young Gus, don't spoil the arrangement. You
know how bad it gets if you move the decimal point when he's
in the middle of something.'

'He does look very bad-tempered,' said Geoffrey.

'He'll spit at you as soon as look at you and I don't think
you want to start collecting *that*,' said Mister Pontoon. 'He's
very particular about his floating-point integers. So we'll move
on now, if you don't mind. Now, look over there: that's the
Coat-Hanger Elk from No Thingfjord. It's called that because

its antlers make wonderful coat hangers. Shame really, there's not many left in the wild. If you want to have one, you have to obtain a special permit and allow it to live in your wardrobe. It can get a bit whiffy, but you'll always know where your best suit is.'

'Ah, I think we've timed it just right here,' said Mister Pontoon. 'Wait for it . . . Oh, straight in the bag! Very neat, young Gus. Now, see that pond, we think we've got one of the famous Chameleon Alligators from Genua. Could be a log, mind you, because it hasn't moved in a long while. But every now and then we see a few feathers near it and Bert, one of the other keepers, reckoned he left a pair of rubber boots on the bank over there last week and they went missing.' Geoffrey peered at the log doubtfully. 'Don't you get too close, young Geoffrey, the paperwork can be a real trial and we already owe Igor for sorting out old Bert when he put his— Well, he got too close to the rotating nogo cage and I shall say no more with a lady present. Now, can you hear that noise?'

Geoffrey stopped and listened; in the distance he detected a boingy sort of sound.

'That comes from the Bouncing Kangaroo enclosure just around the corner. Let's make our way over. They come all the way from Fourecks, and they think that we don't know that they're digging a hole under that trampoline to try to get home. Won't get them anywhere, though; his lordship had us build a metal cage under the enclosure.'

Out of the corner of his eye Geoffrey spotted a small

hunched-over kangaroo making a furtive dash towards an unfeasibly tall and precarious-looking pile of straw and earth in the corner of the enclosure. Mister Pontoon noticed it, too. 'Catch them on the hop if you can, Gus, there's a good lad.'

'Do the animals often escape?' asked Geoffrey earnestly, fearful that potential exhibits for his poo collection might be about to hop off over the fence.

'Not often, but look across there at our troupe of Acrobatic Meerkats. They're always trying to escape too— them and their three-ringed circus. It's not even as if they can juggle very well. We could never keep them in their old cage because they'd form themselves into a pyramid, the one at the top would throw himself across the gap and the others would climb over and out of the top. Later on they'd send a little postcard.'

Geoffrey watched the cartwheeling meerkats for a minute.

'Dreadful show-offs, your meerkats,' said Mister Pontoon. 'No, please don't applaud, it only encourages them. Better be quick in there, Gus, or they'll start their clown routine and you know what Lord Vetinari thinks about clowns.'

As they walked away, some of the meerkats paraded round the cage holding up a badly painted sign that said The Incomparable Meerkats!, and underneath: Performances every 5 minits!

'Isn't that amazing?' said Geoffrey.

The keeper shrugged. 'I don't think so. Sometimes they spell "performance" wrong.'

The
Incomparable Meerkats!
Performances every 5 minits!

As they moved on, Mister Pontoon put his finger to his lips. 'Now hush, walk as quietly as you can, otherwise you won't see a thing. You wait outside with the wheelbarrow, Gus, I'll call you if there's anything to pick up.'

They entered a darkened shed with a large caged area to one side. 'Here we have the last breeding pair of Bashful Pandas from the Agatean Empire,' the keeper whispered. Geoffrey peered into the gloom. He could make out two large shapes sitting at opposite ends of the cage with their backs to the far wall. One of them seemed to be smoking a pipe and the other seemed to be knitting something. 'We're not holding our breath,' said Mister Pontoon, 'but it's a funny old world. And you're in luck—they've not got round to hiding their poo yet. Shy about all their bodily functions, they are, and, just like them, their poo comes out in black and white. Come along, Gus, bring in the shovel.'

'This must be very rare poo indeed,' said Geoffrey.

'It most certainly is,' said Mister Pontoon, 'and if they don't get round to producing a Bashful Panda baby soon there won't be any more of it. So you take good care of it.'

'I certainly will,' said Geoffrey.

'Mister Pontoon?' said Grandmama. 'I wonder if I might make a suggestion. Why don't you just leave them in peace, you know, with a curtain or something? Or maybe some light music? I have no reason to get coarse with my grandson here, all ears, but I think that might be the way forward, as it were.'

'Ooh, are you a biologist, madam?'

'No, but I am a married woman and a married woman who is telling you to give these creatures some privacy. Then I guarantee you will reap dividends and, indeed, pandas.'

'How did all these animals get here?' asked Geoffrey inquisitively.

'They were mostly given as presents to his lordship from visiting indignitaries and ambassadors and the like,' said Mister Pontoon. 'A bit silly, really, because I reckon he'd prefer a nice book, but it's become a bit of a tradition, see. You know, heads of state giving each other animals they don't want. I can still remember the Sultan of Ymitury

turning up with half a dozen creatures bound up in black cloth like oversized skittles. He told us to keep them warm and they would hatch out into giant butterflies. It took us a while to work out that they were his less-favoured concubines.'

'What's a concubine?' asked Geoffrey.

Before the keeper could answer, Grandmama interjected in a voice of thunder, 'It's a kind of vegetable.'

'Are there any animals that I can feed?' asked Geoffrey.

'We've got some Woolly Goats from the Trollbone Mountains,' said the keeper. 'Mind you, it's not easy to tell them front from back at this time of year. Though old Bert is quite clever with them: he waits until they fart and that gives him a clue as to which end to feed.'

In their enclosure Geoffrey studied the incredibly hairy goats and, being an observant boy, and having a special interest, he looked at the ground and saw a pile of droppings. He duly collected these in his bucket and then walked to the other end with the handful of cabbage leaves the keeper had given him. He was rewarded with a long leathery tongue shooting out of the hairy thatch and taking the leaves out of his hand.

'There must be an awful lot of poo every day,' said Geoffrey as the small party walked back towards the gate. 'The compost heaps would be as big as a mountain if you kept it all.'

'Anything we can't use is taken away by Sir Harry King's men; his lordship has a daily collection. Sir Harry pays us a bit extra if we keep the lion dung separate, so lucky for you I can give you a sample of that. It's a bit pongy, mind.'

'Do you have a hippo or a wyvern in the menagerie?'

'No,' said Mister Pontoon, 'they're your heraldics, a different kettle of fish altogether, as it were, most exotic. There's only one place you'll find them, young Geoffrey, and that is at the Royal College of Heralds. They've rebuilt most of it since the fire but it's a strange old place. You'll have a job getting in there: you've got to be nobby before they'll even answer the door. Apart from sirs and lords, the only other person I know who can get in is Doughnut Jimmy the vet. He looks after our animals and was called in there to look at their wyvern only last week.'

'Thank you very much for helping me, Mister Pontoon,' said Geoffrey.

'My pleasure, young man, and it's made a nice change for young Gus. I'll get him to pack up your specimens and we'll put them on top of the carriage because I don't suppose your grandmama will want to travel with that lot inside.'

'I think we should go and have our picnic in the park; it's a bit smelly in here, Geoffrey,' said Grandmama after they had said their farewells.

And so they walked across a large area of lawn and trees, and under one particular tree Geoffrey saw a rather elderly and portly man sitting on a small stool. He was wearing a keeper's hat but Geoffrey couldn't see any animals. Geoffrey edged closer and very politely asked the keeper what he was keeping. 'My job, young sir,' said the man, 'is of fundamental importance in this whole menagerie, because I, young sir, am the Re-Director.'

'The Re-Director?' said Geoffrey. 'That sounds very important. What do you re-direct?'

At Geoffrey's feet and stretching for quite some distance was a thin stone trough filled with greenish water. 'That,' said the old keeper, 'is one of the greatest achievements in engineering by the late and some would say unlamented B. S. Johnson, engineer, architect, and scholar. And that, young sir, is the most unusual and peculiar fish stream in the entire world.'

Geoffrey stood on the edge of the narrow strip and saw a shape in the depths below, slowly moving towards him.

'Stand back now, young sir,' said the keeper, rising to his feet as the shape drew near to where he was sitting. 'This re-directing requires years of experience.' He picked up off the grass a most peculiar object. It was a large net, quite narrow but with a long and sturdy handle. It fitted perfectly into the channel and with a great effort the keeper plunged the net into the water, levered forth a very large, rectangular fish, and then, stepping over the trough and turning hubwards, he placed the fish, this time facing the other way, back into the stream. He heaved the dripping net over his shoulder, lit his pipe, and walked slowly to the other end of the stream where there was another small canvas stool with a parasol attached.

'How often do you have to do this?' Geoffrey asked the back of the receding figure.

'Forty-eight and a half times a day, young sir.'

'What is the half time?' asked Geoffrey.

'Well, the fish and me aren't getting any younger and so sometimes we just goes halfway. And once a week,' said the keeper, 'I do a bit of cleaning out after the fish has done his business.'

'So where do you put the business?' asked Geoffrey.

'Ah, well, young sir, fish business is not as useful for

gardeners as most businesses are, but if you look carefully when you walk away, you will see the trees behind my chairs are slightly bigger than the rest of the trees in the park.'

Before he went to bed that evening Geoffrey carefully put a piece of fruit cake that he'd managed to smuggle up from the kitchen on the windowsill for Old Pediment the gargoyle.

A LUNCH AT THE GUILD OF
PLUMBERS AND DUNNAKIN DIVERS

Like all children, Geoffrey woke at dawn with every switch in his body turned full on. Older people generally check to see that nothing has fallen off in the night. There is always a careful but thorough audit of which limb to get out of bed first so the rest of the body can follow. Geoffrey, however, simply bounded out of bed and, after saying hello to the gleaming Mister Gazunder, went straight to the window to see if the cake had gone. It had, and Geoffrey, being of an observant mind and now informed in the ways of the world of digestion, climbed out onto the ledge to look downwards. He was overjoyed when he saw what he took to be a small deposit on the border of the flower bed beneath his window. Without a thought he raced down the stairs, past an astonished Hartley, out through the back door—pausing only to pick up his bucket from the top step—and round the corner of the house, looking up until he was standing under his bedroom window. It was only then, looking down, that he realized he was barefoot. Luckily, gargoyle poo so much resembles gravel that you may think of it as gravel. Geoffrey was thankful to see he had not stepped in all of it and there was still enough to scrape up into his bucket.

As he made his way back round to the scullery door, finding along the way some long grass on which to wipe his toes, he saw at the end of the garden two burly men hoisting onto their shoulders a pole from which hung a large container. A gentle morning breeze brought a whiff of the privy and he was about to go wandering off following his nose, as it were, when Hartley the cook came to the door and in a kindly voice said, 'Now you come here, young man. Get washed and dressed and your breakfast will be ready when you come down.'

After breakfast Geoffrey took his bucket of gargoyle poo down to the sheds to put in his museum, hoping to see Plain Old Humphrey. Sure enough, he found the gardener sitting on a bench at the bottom of the garden, carefully cleaning his spade. There was no sign of the men Geoffrey had seen earlier, but there was still a whiff hanging around like a smelly ghost. 'Plain Old Humphrey? Who were those men here early this morning?' asked Geoffrey.

'That was Jimmer and Bob, the gongers. They should have been here last night,' said Plain Old Humphrey, 'but

their cart got clamped down at The Soake so they were running a bit late.'

'What do gongers do?' asked Geoffrey.

'Jimmer and Bob work for Sir Harry King and they empty all the cesspits and privies around here,'* said Plain Old Humphrey.

'I know about privies, but I don't know what a cesspit is,' said Geoffrey, determined to get to the bottom of this mysterious occupation.

'Well, using these newfangled lavatory contraptions, like the Deluge Supreme your grandmama has installed, means there is a lot of water in with the business. It all goes into a pit where the water can soak away and then every now and then you have to dig out what's left, and I'm sure your grandmama wouldn't want to do that.'

'And it all goes to Sir Harry?' asked Geoffrey.

'Yes, Sir Harry has collecting carts waiting all round the city to take this valuable night soil down to his yard.'

'I wish I could go to his yard!' said Geoffrey enthusiastically. 'He must have the biggest collection of poo in the world!'

'Watch out, here's trouble,' said Plain Old Humphrey. As he spoke, Lily the maid appeared.

---

* Working at night, gongers, or gongfermors, are sometimes known as 'nightmen.' It requires a steady hand, nerves of steel, and the sense of smell of a turnip to do this job, although the rewards can be great: just consider what may be lost down a privy at night with the only light a candle flame guttering in the wind. I mean, who's going to notice if a locket has gone or even a ring slipped from a cold finger in those conditions? Where there's muck, there's brass, as they used to say, or even better than brass, if you're lucky.

'Your grandmama has been looking all over for you, young man,' she said to Geoffrey. 'You're to come straight inside.' She turned on her heel and walked away without waiting for a reply. Plain Old Humphrey winked at Geoffrey, took his pipe out of his mouth, and poked his tongue out at the retreating figure.

Geoffrey giggled but obediently followed Lily into the kitchen, where he found his grandmama, who was talking to Hartley the cook. 'Geoffrey and I will be out for lunch, but we will be back for dinner,' she was saying. 'Geoffrey—oh there you are—we have been invited to a luncheon at the Guild of Plumbers and Dunnakin Divers by my good friend Sir Charles Lavatory, so you'll need to look smart. I've bought you a new jacket; it's in your room. Please don't ruin this one because I've had it tailored especially for you.'

Geoffrey ran upstairs and was delighted to find his new jacket had at least eight pockets, and they were all lined with a rubbery material that looked as though nothing could stain or even seep through to the sur-face. How kind of Grandmama, he thought. I could collect a lot of interesting stuff wearing this jacket.

Their carriage took them up Nonesuch Street, along Park Lane, past the Opera House,

and across the Brass Bridge to the Street of Alchemists, where the coach stopped outside the grand entrance to the Plumbers' Guild, which had a bellpull that looked just like the chain and lever on Grandmama's water closet and a door knocker that was shaped like a long-handled spade with a rounded end.

Grand as the entrance was, nothing prepared Geoffrey for the sight that greeted them when they went in. The room was vast and the walls were completely covered from floor to ceiling with shiny patterned tiles. There were large pictures, also made up of tiles, of serious men with expressions of stern contentment and jobs well done.

'How nice to see you, Maud, and this must be your grandson Geoffrey.' A tall, grey-haired, distinguished-looking man with muttonchop whiskers approached, greeting Grandmama with a bow, and a smile for Geoffrey.

'This, Geoffrey, is Sir Charles Lavatory,' said Grandmama.

Geoffrey shook Sir Charles's hand politely like a pupil meeting his master.

'Now, Geoffrey, in accordance with the rules of the Guild of Plumbers and Dunnakin Divers, you need to wash your hands, and I shall do the same.' Sir Charles pointed to a long line of shiny sinks along one wall, many in constant use as one plumber greeted another. The air had the deliciously sharp smell of lye soap.

Ablutions completed, Sir Charles then led Geoffrey and Grandmama into a lounge, where a number of other gentlemen were seated together in small groups.

'Sir Charles,' said Geoffrey. 'Do you mind if I ask whether you like having the name of Lavatory?'

For a moment the hubbub of noise from conversations around them fell silent as the whole room listened. Every eye was watching Sir Charles, whose face was at first blank and then all smiles.

'What an excellent question!' he cried. 'To tell you the truth, young man, as you may expect, I was teased a lot when I went to school, but as they say, that which does not kill you makes you stronger. And so, as soon as I could, with the help of my late father, I set to work to make the lavatory the marble marvel of the age and a boon and blessing to all mankind. I can truly say that I have ended up flushed with pride, now knowing that the name is associated with satisfaction and ease.' To his surprise, Geoffrey saw a small tear form in the corner of Sir Charles's eye as he continued: 'There are times of an evening when I go down to the workshops, all silent, and look at the work that's going on on this year's model, with the seat warmer and the patented straining bars, and I can't help thinking that I've done my best for mankind. I wonder how many men with hands cleaner than mine can say that.'

Every seat in the house was vacated as the plumbers got to their feet and clapped their scrupulously clean hands together until the echoes piled up. When it had all died away and conversations around the room restarted, Sir Charles took Geoffrey by the hand and said, 'Now, come with me, Geoffrey, there is someone here whom I know you would like to meet and who, I think, would very much like to meet you as well.'

They walked into the large dining room, which was filled with tables laid ready for lunch. Already sitting at one was a large, red-faced man with short, wiry grey hair and a grizzled beard. Geoffrey couldn't help noticing the big golden rings on every finger and the large golden chain around his neck. 'I'd like to introduce you, young man, to Sir Harry King,' said Sir Charles.

Geoffrey was speechless with delight and awe.

'It's not like you to have nothing to say,' said Grandmama, chivvying him forward. 'I must tell you, Sir Harry, Geoffrey has a very keen interest in something dear to your heart, that is to say, muck in all its various ramifications.'

'Then come and sit beside me, young Geoffrey, and tell me all about it,' said Sir Harry in a gruff voice. Sir Harry was a man with daughters and granddaughters, none of whom really wanted to know anything about the source of the family fortune that they enjoyed.

'Well,' began Geoffrey, 'I am very interested in poo and I've got this museum in Grandmama's garden with thirty-seven different sorts of poo and I'm trying to collect specimens from every animal in the world so that people will come and visit and they'll be able to see rare and unusual poo.'

'Well,' said Sir Harry, 'I am so pleased to find a young man like you keen to make his way in the world, seeing that so many young men are skivers and slackers. But I have to tell you, Geoffrey, that I'm not sure there's a living to be made out of simply collecting poo samples. I made my money in the bulk market by collecting poo from people who simply wanted to get rid of it—even paid me to take it away—and then selling it on to other people who could find a use for it.'

'Do you collect from the Royal College of Heralds?'

'I expect so,' said Sir Harry, who had an instinct for when a question was more than just a polite enquiry. 'Was there something in particular you wanted?'

'Well, I need wyvern poo and hippo poo. Mister Pontoon said that only sirs and lords and nobs can get in there, and sometimes the vet is allowed in when they need help with the wyvern.'

'I think I can help you there,' said Sir Harry with a smile.

'In fact, I have an appointment to visit them this afternoon to discuss my coat of arms. And if your grandmama allows it, you could always come with me.' He winked at Grandmama.

'May I go, Grandmama, may I?' asked Geoffrey. 'Please? Please? Please?'

'If you promise to behave yourself and do what Sir Harry tells you and not bother the staff too much, then I think it would be fine.'

At this point large tureens of soup were brought to the table, shaped very much like outsize chamber pots emblazoned with the guild's coat of arms. For the first time Geoffrey looked properly around the room. A large sideboard ran

along one wall with great silver candlesticks and buckets and strange-shaped bowls and platters laid upon it. More pictures of serious men with forbidding beards lined the wall and there was a list of names in gold paint under the heading Presidents of the Guild.

A magnificent pie, that was served in a very deep dish reminiscent of a bucket, with lots of good gravy, followed the soup. But for Geoffrey the real treat was a huge trifle, just like Cook made, but presented here in a crystal dish modelled on one of Sir Charles's recent creations.

'Now, Geoffrey, before you go off with Sir Harry,' Grandmama warned, 'I think you ought to visit the cloakroom.' Geoffrey went in the direction indicated and found a large mahogany door with brass handles and a sign saying Gentlemen. Inside, shining white tiles covered the walls, floor, and ceiling. Geoffrey felt as though he were in a giant upturned sink. A row of hand basins decorated with flowers ran along one wall, and opposite them stood a row of cubicles. Inside these were water closets grander even than

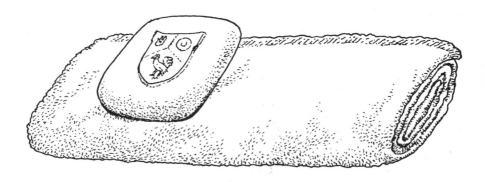

Grandmama's, with huge brass cisterns above flowery china bowls and polished copper pipes.

Geoffrey washed his hands with the soap provided, noticing that even that had the guild coat of arms on it, then dried them on the spotless white fluffy towel.

'That's a very grand cloakroom,' he said to Sir Harry as he emerged.

'I'll tell you this, young man,' said Sir Harry. 'The men who do the dirtiest jobs are always the cleanest whenever that is possible, and it is only right they should have the very best for themselves.'

'Goodness!' said Geoffrey. 'I expect that means that you must have an even grander cloakroom.'

'Personally, I'm not too worried,' said Harry, 'but Lady King has what she calls her en suites and I'm not allowed in the house without walking through a tray of disinfectant. Now, it's coming up to the time of my appointment at the Royal College of Heralds,' he said, turning to Grandmama. 'I'll drop your boy home when we're done, if that's all right, ma'am. It's just around the corner from you.'

They travelled in Sir Harry's coach, which was painted a dark and glossy green with the letters H and K in shiny gold leaf on the doors. Fortunately for Geoffrey there was enough ventilation for him to escape the very worst of Harry King's very large cigar.*

---

* Harry King smoked cigars all the time, apparently, but given the way he earned his money, the acrid cigar smoke probably counted as fresh air.

As they turned the corner by the Palace, Sir Harry remarked, 'See that, Geoffrey? My lads collect not far short of a tonne a week there. Not much paperwork to speak of because his lordship expects his employees to bring their own—and he expects me to do the collecting pro bono.'

'What does pro bono mean?' asked Geoffrey.

'For nothing, lad; free, gratis, goodwill. Still, mustn't

grumble. At least we've got a ruler who understands the worth of your workingman.'

They had now reached Pseudopolis Yard, and, gesturing towards the Opera House, Sir Harry continued: 'Even though the performers don't eat very much, that place gets through so much fizzy wine it's a golden river in its own right, and that, my boy, is why they call me King of the Golden River.'

'Sorry, Sir Harry,' said Geoffrey. 'I don't know what you mean.'

Harry King smiled and said, 'Well, lad, there's poo, isn't there? And there's piss! And, to tell you the truth, I started my career leaving buckets outside every public house for people to piss in, and me and my lads would take them away when they were full. And we would sell it. Amazing stuff. I mean, it's almost alchemical really. It's astonishing what you can get out of it, even explosives if you're careful—but don't worry about that yourself, of course, it never actually happens while you're doing it.'

As the journey progressed, every now and then Sir Harry would bang on the roof of the coach with his stick and give the driver instructions to either detour round the back of a building or turn off into an alley and stop near one of his collection points, where he would lean out of the window to make sure everything was in order. He seemed to know everyone by name and his gruff voice cut through the clamour of the street straight into the unfragrant ears of his employees. 'Just you clean up that spillage, Jake,' he shouted to a young man trying to kick something into the gutter. 'That's money straight down the drain, that is!'

Just as the Royal College of Heralds came into view in the distance, Sir Harry said, 'And after the piss pots I realized that there was money to be made in the things that people were throwing away. Everything. There's always someone who could use something, and they have to get it from Harry King.'

They drew up at the large green gates, stepped down from the coach, and rang the bell. A small wicket gate in the main door was opened by a liveried porter, who asked them their business. 'I have an appointment with the Herald, smart boy,' said Sir Harry, taking his cigar out of his mouth. 'To discuss the progress of my coat of arms.'

'Which herald would that be?' asked the doorman, seeming a little unnerved.

'Search me,' said Harry. 'Something like, er, reddish breakfast roll?'

The porter let them into the courtyard and Geoffrey looked around. It was much smaller than he expected, but quite smelly. In the middle was a muddy pond with a couple of hippos wallowing in it, and a small owl was perched on the handle of an old broom leaning against the wall.

'If you would like to come this way, Sir Harold,' said the returning porter, 'we have a design mapped out for your approval. And is there anything we can do to help your young friend?' he asked, eyeing Geoffrey.

'Oh, I expect he'll find something to do around here,

he likes the animals,' said Sir Harry, giving Geoffrey a big wink. 'Very studious boy, this young lad, very interested in what you gentlemen would call, I suspect, animal excrement.'

'I'll let old Joseph keep an eye on the young man. He cleans the yard for us and knows his way around all the pens,' said the porter, leading Sir Harry away.

A small elderly man, his head bent forward, emerged slowly from a shed and, transferring the owl to his shoulder, took hold of the broom, which he used as a support to walk across the yard. 'Can I help you clean the animals' cages?' asked Geoffrey, seeing a definite poo opportunity.

'Well, I've been round the hippos,' said the old man, 'but they'll probably start again soon. You could give me a hand with the wyvern if you like, he always needs scraping out.'

Geoffrey and the old man walked towards a cage where a miserable-looking creature lay slumped on damp straw.

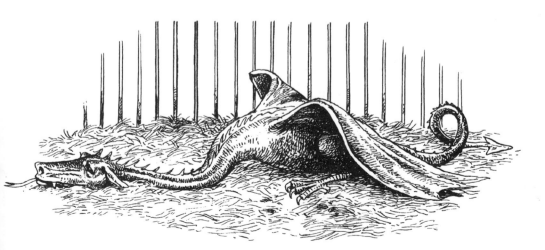

'Here, use this,' said the old man, handing Geoffrey a flat wooden shovel. Just scrape his doings into that bucket there.'

Geoffrey did as instructed and contrived at the same time to get a small amount of the surprisingly green poo into one of his lined pockets.

They wandered slowly back towards the hippos. 'Oh no, here we go, look out,' said Joseph. 'Mind your back against the wall, just stand with me in the corner here and we should be all right.'

Geoffrey watched with amazement as one of the hippos emerged from the pond and started whirling his short tail round like a windmill, spraying poo in a wide arc.*

'Goodness, do they always do that?' asked Geoffrey.

'Mostly they do,' said the old man. 'I cleans up what I can, but sometimes I can't reach because it goes so high.'

Geoffrey looked at the wall behind him and sure enough there were lumps of dried hippo poo plastered across the stones above him. The old man pushed the broom across the yard. 'I'll move what I can now,' he said, 'because once it sets it's a bugger to shift.' Geoffrey managed to dislodge a dried lump and secrete it in another of his jacket pockets.

He looked hopefully at the morpork still sitting on the

---

* Hippos really are the most dangerous of animals, and at both ends. Not only can they move very quickly to close their jaws on the unwary swimmer, but they can go on to spray any unfortunate onlooker with poo by whirling their tails like propellers as they excrete. Zoologists would say that this is behaviour designed to mark their territory. The author thinks that it is one of nature's more interesting jokes.

old man's shoulder. The owl, somehow knowing what was required, hunched down and obliged by doing a poo, which landed on the old man's back.

'Oh dear,' said Geoffrey, suppressing a smile, 'that owl's done a poo on your jacket. Would you like me to wipe it off?'

He was just scraping his morpork specimen into yet another pocket when Sir Harry emerged into the yard. 'Ready to go, Geoffrey?' Sir Harry asked, taking in the scene.

'Yes, thank you,' said Geoffrey. And so they climbed into the coach and swiftly set off for Nonesuch Street.

'Well, you certainly take your hobby seriously, young man,' said Sir Harry. 'I like a boy with purpose. How would you like to visit my yard tomorrow? I'll send a coach to pick you up bright and early and we can go down the river together in my launch.'

'I'd like that more than anything in the world,' said Geoffrey enthusiastically.

'Very well. We'll check with Grandmama when we drop you off,' said Sir Harry.

Grandmama came to the door as they arrived back home. 'That is most kind of you, Sir Harry,' she said, when Sir Harry proposed tomorrow's outing. 'I know Geoffrey has become very interested in your enterprise while he has been staying here in Ankh-Morpork, and as his visit's coming to an end it's a very good opportunity for him. Geoffrey, I think you probably need to take your new acquisitions into your museum, don't you? And emphatically refrain from leaving them anywhere in the house,' she added, her nose twitching in distaste. 'And while you're there, ask Plain Old Humphrey to help you wash out your pockets with Doctor Painforth's Hygienic Restorative.'

AN ADVENTURE WITH
SIR HARRY KING

The doorbell rang at 9 a.m. and Geoffrey raced to pick up his jacket and find Widdler's lead. Sir Harry was standing outside on the top step, smoking a fat cigar and wearing a tall stovepipe hat and a coat with a velvet collar. He greeted Geoffrey with a wide smile and a puff of smoke. 'Are you ready to see Harry's world, young man? We'll walk down to the Linnet Landing today; it's a lovely morning and it's no distance.'

'Please may I bring Widdler?' asked Geoffrey hopefully, indicating the little dog, who was wagging his tail expectantly.

'Good name for a dog that,' said Sir Harry with a laugh. 'I don't see why not, but be sure you keep him on a lead. And any little deposit he makes on my property belongs to

me, especially if it's white. The tanners love white,' he said with a wink.

As the trio walked up Nonesuch Street Sir Harry kept a close eye on the ground, using his stick to turn over the occasional pile of leaves in the gutter. Off in the distance a boy was assiduously scraping something into a bucket. As they approached, Geoffrey recognized Louis and waved at him. 'That's my friend Louis! I helped him collect dog poo in the park. He works for you, doesn't he?'

'Yes, good lad that, works hard and knows his stuff. He'll go far. Here, Louis, go back up to number sixty-four, there's a little white pearl there as bright as a penny. And you know what, it's got your name on it. Be quick before some other bugger gets it.'

'Thank you, Sir Harry,' said Louis, disappearing up the road.

They reached the river, where Sir Harry's boat, *Lady Euphemia*, was moored at the landing. It was a large rowing boat with three liveried oarsmen and a coxswain at the stern. At the bow was a covered area with several seats, and amidships several large steel-lined wooden bins with a collection of nets, hooks, and grappling irons alongside. 'Just in case I see anything along the way I think should be mine,' said Sir Harry, lighting another cigar.

They cast off, the coxswain negotiating the craft into the main channel of the river. Sir Harry changed his hat for a nautical peaked cap emblazoned with the word 'captain' and a small embroidered anchor. He took the large seat in

the centre, all the while looking around to see who and what was floating in his vicinity. There was a bell beside him so he could attract the coxswain's attention to give him instructions, via a speaking tube, as to any change of course.

Geoffrey had never travelled in a boat before and to be there with Sir Harry was his best adventure yet. There was a lot to see: the river was very busy with barges and small ferries and water taxis. He reached over and made to dangle his fingers in the brown sludge.

'I'd keep your hands out of the water if I were you,' warned Sir Harry. 'Are you enjoying youself?'

'Oh, yes,' said Geoffrey. 'At home I don't get to see anything like this.'

'So what do you do to amuse yourself?' asked Sir Harry.

'Well, I've got lots of toys. I like playing with my soldiers and Papa bought me a Captain Carrot last Hogswatch, though I really wanted the Omnian Quisition game.'

'When I was a lad we had to make our own amusement,' said Harry. 'On rainy days if we couldn't play foot-the-ball and if we were lucky, and in the right place at the right time, we might spot a brace of floaters coming down in the gutters. Oh, we used to have some fun wagering which one would hit the grating first. Like men-o'-war they were, a convoy of pure delight for us kids. We called it poo sticks.'

As they approached the Ankh Bridge the coxswain shouted, 'Umbers up, lads.' The oarsmen, who could not see where they were going, but only where other people had been, without breaking their rhythm pulled up a large tarpaulin canopy over their heads.

'Folks think it's funny to take a potty shot at me and my boat,' said Sir Harry. 'They didn't laugh so much the day I took a marksman with a crossbow along for the ride. There's still a few fools that can't sit comfortably for trying it on with Harry King.'

He saw the expression on Geoffrey's face and said, 'Don't worry, it was only rock salt. They'll get better when it works off.'

They continued downriver, where on either side there were tall warehouses and queues of barges waiting to be unloaded. Large sailing ships were anchored by the wharves, and lighters and other small craft darted to and fro on the scummy, barely moving water. Occasionally, a warning shout of 'Watch out below' was to be heard as the stevedores scurried over a ship like ants. Suddenly Sir Harry leapt to his feet. 'By Offler's tooth, lad, we've got a couple,' he cried, pointing out a pair of floaters. 'Look, there, I'll bet you a dollar to a penny that the one nearer the bank will hit that wall first.'

With a practised eye they both studied the movement of their movements in the current.

'Ah, well, I reckon that one's yours, lad; I'll settle up with you later. And thank you very much for letting an old man revisit his boyhood for a while.'

As they rowed through the ancient portal of the River Gate, Sir Harry was hailed by a group of watchmen who were huddled smoking in the lee of one of the old battlements. 'Any chance of an extra pickup, Sir Harry?' one of them shouted. 'Trap four is full and some of the lads had a Klatchian last night.'

'What? I'm the bloody boss, ain't I,' said Harry angrily. 'There's one of my lighters along in about fifteen minutes, they'll help you out.'

Outside the city walls the view changed to ramshackle sheds and old farmhouses, reedy swamps and a towpath. 'Not far now,' said Sir Harry. 'You can just see the top of my biggest heap, over there.'

Geoffrey looked afresh at what he'd taken to be a small hill in the distance. As they drew nearer he could see smoke rising, and the general miasma of smells grew much more concentrated. They came to what looked like a small city of shacks and lean-tos. 'I let some of my workers live there free,' said Sir Harry. 'It means they're always willing to make an effort and squeeze out the last drop, so to speak, and they're never late for work.'

The boat turned towards a landing quay, where the

oarsmen helped Geoffrey, who was carrying Widdler under his arm, to disembark.

'Now hold my hand, lad,' said Sir Harry. 'There's a lot going on; you need to keep your wits about you.'

A maze of moving belts crisscrossed the vast yard and carts were being loaded and unloaded from various bins and heaps of rubbish. Above Geoffrey's head pulleys with rows of buckets rattled along on heavy chains. The whole world around him seemed to be moving and, from the stink,

Geoffrey guessed it was mainly poo on the move. There were two golems working on giant treadmills and more golems and trolls and humans and goblins working at the moving belts. Every now and then one of them would reach out, pick something off the belt, and put it into one of several bins alongside them. Gnolls, with brushes and buckets and wearing muzzles over their mouths to stop them eating everything in sight—including the brush—were clearing anything that fell from the great creaking edifice.

Geoffrey and Sir Harry climbed some steep stairs to Sir Harry's office, which was like a crow's nest with windows all around, designed so that he could see everything that was going on in every corner of his empire.

'I've a couple of jobs I need to attend to,' said Sir Harry, 'so I'll get my foreman to give you a guided tour and I'll join you later.'

Sir Harry opened one of the windows and, looking down, shouted, 'Barker? Come on up here if you please, I've a job for you.' He then held out a pair of stout waders. 'Right, you better put these boots on, Geoffrey, and it's probably best if you leave little Widdler in my office. I've got dogs down there that would have him for lunch.'

A short man with a broad grin but unsmiling, steely eyes came up the steps to the office. He was wearing a flat cap, a much-patched tweedy jacket, a big leather apron tied up with string, and long boots. He looked at Geoffrey as if calculating how much he'd be worth in his component parts.

'Would you show my young friend around the works for

me, Barker? He's a keen student of the world of waste. Make sure he comes to no harm and keep him well away from the thaumic dump,' warned Sir Harry as he picked up his overcoat and disappeared down the stairs.

'What's the thaumic dump, Mister Barker?' asked Geoffrey, as they descended into the maelstrom of the busy yard.

'That's where we store waste from the University. We have to keep it in a lead-lined pit or it gets out and crawls all over the place. Sir Harry doesn't mind having it here because it generates so much heat, so it's never cold down here, even in winter. Admittedly things walk around on their own, but I suppose that's progress, that is.'

'Where exactly is it?' asked Geoffrey, looking around keenly.

'More than my job's worth to take you there,' said Barker, shaking his head. 'We'll start at goods inwards, shall we? You stay close beside me, don't talk to anyone, and don't pick up anything. And I mean *anything*, right?'

They made their way, through large gates guarded by trolls and big fierce dogs, to the riverside, where men were shovelling the cargo from the barges into the backs of carts.

'Right, as you see, most solid waste comes in by river these days and it's all taken by cart to the moving belts for sorting.'

Geoffrey's eyes were everywhere. 'How do you know where it's all come from?' he asked.

'Barge master's got a docket, but we can usually tell by the colour and smell. After you've worked here a few years you get to know if it's from the privies in the Shades or down

The Soake or from the Park Lane cesspits. It's all down to diet in the end: what goes in must come out. This barge is from the Cable Street area, that's mostly dwarfs, very concentrated and compact, needs to stand a bit before we can use it. The other problem is that some of the deep-downers use fine chain mail for the paperwork, and if a few links drop in and aren't picked out it causes merry hell with the grinding machine.'

They walked back into the yard and Barker pointed to a covered area where several people with clipboards were walking up and down a long trestle table, making notes and occasionally sniffing the contents of long-handled, saucer-like containers. 'Over there are the nosers,' he said. 'They can tell, almost to the street, where the stuff comes from and what's in it, then they can blend the right mix to go to the tanners or the dyers or perfume makers or whatever. Clever blokes. And you see that big heap of fish bones? That's come from the Temple of Offler; it's been a big feast day up there. And over here is the remains of last year's beetroot festival that the folks from Uberwald staged. The tanners had a real problem with pink leather until we separated it out for them.'

'What happens to the stuff from the menagerie?' asked Geoffrey.

'We keep that separate, too, that comes under exotics, along with the stuff from the College of Heralds. Good thing is, the elephant poo is bagged up and sold for compost as soon as it comes in, otherwise it'd take over the place.'

As Geoffrey and Barker walked along by one of the moving belts, Sir Harry joined them again. He'd taken off his hat and overcoat and was wearing a brown cotton smock with a row of cigars in the top pocket, a flat cap, and leather boots. 'I hope you're impressed by what you've seen, lad?' he asked.

Before Geoffrey could answer, a dwarf climbed up to a platform in the centre of the yard and blew an enormous horn. 'That's old Helmhammerhand sounding the shift change,' said Sir Harry, looking at his watch. 'It must be time for a spot of lunch. Right, young lad, let's go and see what we have to eat today. On your way up to my office use the facilities. Here's the key, make sure you lock it after you.'

In this lavatory, Geoffrey was interested to see there was a large wad of old newspaper hanging on a hook; but the soap was scented and the towel was clean. He smiled and thought: Sir Harry King doesn't waste anything.

The moment Geoffrey arrived back in the office Sir Harry lifted a large wicker hamper onto his desk, pulled out a packet of sandwiches and two slices of cake, and passed them across.

'And here's a bottle of lemonade and a glass, Geoffrey,' said Sir Harry.

'Are you going to have some?' asked Geoffrey politely.

'No, lad, I'm having a bottle of beer. As for food, I have to tell you, young man, that what I like most is leftovers. I love leftovers and my good lady wife, who has Cook send lunch up every day, has trained her in the art of creating leftovers without the necessity of the posh meal beforehand. *I've* got cold mutton chops with Merkle and Stingbat's very fine brown sauce. Lovely! Tuck in, lad, and then I'll get you taken home.'

'Thank you very much indeed, Sir Harry,' said Geoffrey, finishing every drop of his lemonade so that there would be no leftover. 'It's been a really interesting day and I think I must have seen more poo than any other boy in the world!'

'Well, then, here's a present for you,' said Sir Harry. 'I owe you a dollar for the poo-sticks race, and no doubt young Widdler has been leaving me a few presents around the place, so this here paperweight is a very special item indeed. They call them Pearls of the Pavement; I got young Derek Proust to do me a one-off.' He handed Geoffrey a perfect replica of a small white dog turd in which a large gold dollar was embedded. 'Put this in your museum, lad, it's the only one of its kind and worth a bob or two. I've enjoyed our time together, Geoffrey, and if you ever want to come and work for me, I'd take you like

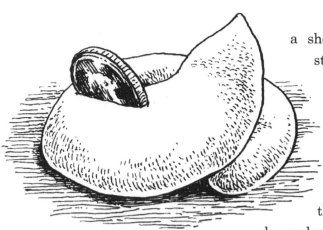

a shot. You'd have to start at the bottom, though,' he said with a wink.

He escorted Geoffrey to where his coach was waiting. 'Take the boy home now,' he ordered the coachman. 'And make sure you see him in the door.' Geoffrey thanked Sir Harry again and waved from the coach until he was out of sight.

As they passed the River Gate guardhouse on their way back into the city, Geoffrey was pleased to see one of Harry King's carts parked outside.

They drove through a busy market and Geoffrey noticed a horse stop in the road. After a day spent with Sir Harry, he had no hesitation in politely asking the coachman to halt so that he could gather some fresh horse apples for Plain Old Humphrey to put on the roses.

When they got home, while the coachman waited, Widdler relieved himself on the gatepost, then Geoffrey picked him up and carried him up the steps to the front door. To his great surprise and delight it was opened by his mama even before he'd pulled the bell.

'I've been looking out for you, Geoffrey!' she cried. 'I've missed you so much.'

Geoffrey knew he was theoretically too old for a kiss, but he threw himself into her arms and she gathered him up. Over her shoulder he saw Grandmama holding a very young baby. 'This is your new sister Holly,' said Grandmama. 'She's very pretty, but she smells a bit. I'll get Nanny to change her, shall I?'

Geoffrey looked at his mama and grandmama. 'Can I help?' he asked, picking up his bucket.

The End

Now don't forget to wash your hands . . .

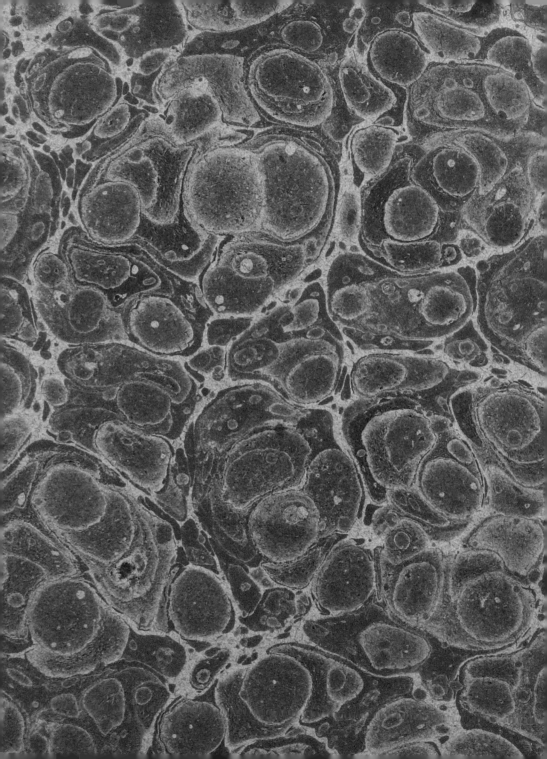